The Wonderful
HibiscOak Tree

Written & Illustrated by
Melissa Wakhu

This book belongs to

____

____

For Tando, Amara, Maisha & Emunah.

ISBN 978 9966 137 35 7

Edited by Maïmouna Jallow

Printed in Nairobi.

First printing, 2019.

DECLISSA Inc.
P.O. BOX 17722-00100
Nairobi, Kenya.

www.declissa.com

Tia is a tiny black seed.
A strong wind has blown her
far away from her mother.

As she's tossed about in the air, she giggles
with excitement about her future. She
is going to do wonderful things!

She soars past a gigantic oak tree. It has
thick lush green leaves and beautiful
birds chirping on its branches.

At once, she decides that she wants to be
big, tall, and leafy just like the oak tree.

Tumbling past a field of
radiant hibiscus flowers, Tia
admires their dazzling colors
and watches the birds as they
gracefully drink their nectar.

At once she decides that she
wants be as mighty as the
oak tree AND as elegant as
the hibiscus flowers.

Softly, she lands onto a warm
and moist patch of earth.

She covers herself under the soil.

It's cozy and comfortable! She begins
to germinate. "Ti hi hi!" she giggles,
"sprouting is so ticklish".

As roots burst out of her and
stems pop through her hard
coat, she beams with joy.

"Oh! Wow! It is happening, I'm
going to be big and beautiful!"

As time passes, Tia keeps
shooting out of the ground and
getting taller every day.

8

She dreams of all the beautiful birds that will
soon perch on her strong branches, building nests
and feeding on the nectar from her flowers.

She even names herself, *The Wonderful HibiscOak Tree!*

Oh-oh! Something is going wrong.
Tia has stopped growing. And she's
only 5 meters tall. An oak tree is at
least five times taller! And to make
matters worse, her bark is brown
and cracked. And thorns have begun
to pop out all over her branches!

"No! No! No!" She cries,
"I don't want this pimply
and thorny body!"

She tries to think tall,
luscious, floral thoughts,
hoping it will help her
become the Wonderful
HibiscOak Tree
she is destined to be.

But thin sharp leaves
sprout next to her
thorns and cover her.

And wispy branches, spread out
of her like long fingers, dangling
clumsily in all directions. The thorns
and thin leaves are multiplying!

Tia is horrified!

No towering canopy.
No lush green leaves.
No Wonderful HibiscOak Tree.

"Sob! With my thin limbs, thorns
and needlelike leaves, no bird
will ever perch on me. They will
be scared of getting poked!"

"I have no elegant flowers, so no nectar
either. I am absolutely nothing! Sob!"

Tia stands alone, feeling forlorn and battered in the wind. Then a brightly colored bird lands on her.

"Why so gloomy?" he chirps as he pecks
and walks on her branch.

Tia, astonished that the bird hasn't been pricked by her thorns, sighs heavily and says, "I have thin leaves and an ugly thorny pimply bark. I was meant to be gigantic like the oak and radiant like the hibiscus. A Wonderful HibiscOak Tree! But now, I'm just a plain wattle tree."

The bird continues pecking.

Then looking at Tia he says,
"You are an Acacia tree. You always have leaves for us
all year round. Your branches are easy to pluck for nests
and the thorns keep us safe. Even the towering giraffe
feed on you. You are beautiful and meaningful to us."

And with a chirp, the bird flies off with a twig.

"I'm an Acacia tree!" Tia says out loud.

"My leaves are beautiful and my thorns and branches
have a purpose!" Soon, several birds are perching and
pecking all over her before flying off again. And before
Tia knows it, more birds come and do the same.

Tia is now beaming and standing tall.
She is not a Wonderful HibiscOak Tree.
She is an Acacia tree!
She is beautiful and meaningful.

The End